Jumping Rope!

GRL: F

Word count: 131

Text type: fiction

Genre: realistic fiction

High-frequency words: *came, can, he, I, in, like, look, said, the*

capstone
classroom

Start Reading (Capstone Classroom) is published by Capstone Press,
1710 Roe Crest Drive, North Mankato, Minnesota 56003.
www.capstoneclassroom.com

Originally published by Wayland, a division of Hachette Children's Books,
a Hachette UK company.
www.hachette.co.uk

[10 9 8 7 6 5 4 3 2 1]
Printed and bound in China.

Jumping Rope!
ISBN 978-1-4765-3206-6

Jumping Rope!

Written by Anna Matthew
Illustrated by Heather Heyworth

capstone
classroom

My sisters and I
like jumping rope.

We play jump rope
together.

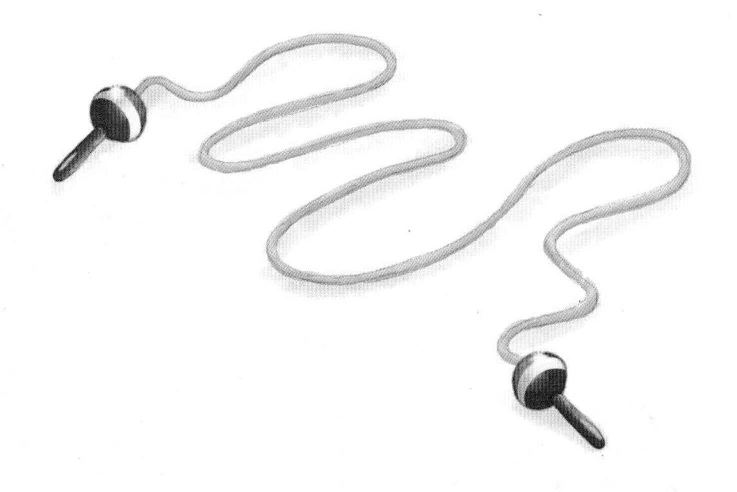

The letter carrier
came along.

"That looks fun. Can
I jump in?" he said.

Then a boy came up
the street.

He liked jumping rope,
so he jumped in.

This is fun!

A man walked up the street.

"That looks fun. Can
I jump in?" he said.

Then the truck driver came along.

He liked jumping rope, so he jumped in.

This is fun!

A garbage collector came up the street.

"Can I jump in?" he said. "I like jumping rope!"

Then a police officer came along.

He looked at us all.

"Don't jump rope in the street!" he said.

So the letter carrier, the boy, the man, the truck driver, and the garbage collector ...

... all went skipping away!

Guide Reading

Jumping Rope!

Before reading, examine the illustrations with children and have children locate the book title and author's name.

Preview the book

Say:
The girl and her sisters like to jump rope. She tells us about the time when lots of people came along and jumped rope too.

> **Let's read the title: *Jumping Rope!***
> **Let's look at the picture on page 5, where the girl and her sisters are jumping rope. Let's take a look through the pictures. Who joins them?**

Continue to page through the book, discussing the illustrations and what they tell readers about the events and characters.

CCSS Use illustrations and details in a story to describe its characters, setting, and events. **(RL.3)**

Focus on fluency

Model how to track print as you read aloud all or part of the text with accuracy and expression. Have children follow your lead, prompting them as necessary to track print, to self-correct, and to use their knowledge of the relationships between letters and sounds to pronounce words and check meaning:

- **I like the way that you check the picture and use the letters to figure out the word. Then you reread the sentence to make sure it all made sense.**
- **Did you see the question mark there? That changes the way that we read and speak. Let's try it again so it sounds like a question.**

CCSS Read with sufficient accuracy and fluency to support comprehension. **(RF.2)**

Focus on high-frequency words: *came, can, he, I, in, like, look, said, the*

Select a high-frequency word and ask children to find it throughout the book.

- Discuss the shapes of the letters and the letter sounds.
- To memorize the word, children can write it in the air and then write it repeatedly on a whiteboard or on paper, leaving a space between each attempt to establish word boundaries.

Have children use the high-frequency words to write or tell about the text.

CCSS Read common high-frequency words by sight. **(RF.3)**

Connect to the Common Core

Jumping Rope!

Prompt children's thinking about *Jumping Rope!* with questions such as the following:

Key Ideas and Details (RL.1, RL.3)

- The girls are jumping rope. Who joins them first? (the letter carrier)
- Why does he join them? (He thinks jumping rope looks like fun.)
- Where does this story take place? (in the street)
- What problem does jumping rope in the street cause? (The police officer does not want so many people to be in the street.)

Craft and Structure (RL.5, RL.6)

- How can you tell that this book tells a story and does not give information? (The book has characters who speak. It has a beginning, middle, and end. It does not tell facts about jumping rope.)
- One of the sisters tells the story. Find a word that helps you know that a sister tells the story. (My sisters and I like jumping rope. He looked at us all.)

Integration of Knowledge and Ideas (RL.7)

- Look at the illustration on page 15. How do the characters feel? How can you tell? (They are happy and having fun. They are smiling and jumping. The garbage collector is smiling at them because they are having so much fun.)

Phonics and Word Recognition (RF.3)

- Say the word *jumping*. How many syllables do you hear? Clap when you say each one: *jump ing*. (two syllables)
- What other words in the story have two syllables? Clap when you say them. (*letter, driver, along, sisters, garbage, police, skipping*)

Writing (W.7)

The police officer asked the people jumping rope to move out of the street. Where is the best place for children to play? Have children make a poster for a playground, a park, a school gym, or somewhere else that is a good place for children to play. They could make posters to hang up in your school and community.